Dora's Book of Manners

by Christine Ricci
illustrated by Susan Hall

Simon Spotlight/Nick Jr.

New York　　London　　Toronto　　Sydney

Based on the TV series *Dora the Explorer*® as seen on Nick Jr.®

SIMON SPOTLIGHT
An imprint of Simon & Schuster Children's Publishing Division
1230 Avenue of the Americas, New York, New York 10020
Copyright © 2004 Viacom International Inc. All rights reserved.
NICKELODEON, NICK JR., *Dora the Explorer*, and all related titles, logos,
and characters are registered trademarks of Viacom International Inc.
All rights reserved, including the right of reproduction in whole or in part in any form.
SIMON SPOTLIGHT and colophon are registered trademarks of Simon & Schuster.
Manufactured in the United States of America
16 18 20 19 17
ISBN 0-689-86533-3

It was a sunny day, and Dora and Boots were playing hide-and-seek in the Flowery Garden.

"I found you!" shouted Dora, pointing up toward the tree.

"I've been caught!" giggled Boots.

Suddenly Dora stopped and listened. "Oh, no! I think I hear someone crying."

Dora and Boots followed the sound over to the teary Grumpy Old Troll.

"Hi, Mr. Troll," said Dora. "Is something wrong?"

"I was very grumpy this morning, *so* grumpy that when my friend, Mouse, came over to play, I told him to go away," replied the Troll. "But now I'm sad. I wasn't very nice to Mouse and I think I hurt his feelings. Can you help me get my best friend back?"

"We can help you, Mr. Troll," replied Dora.

"Great!" said the Troll. "I know some riddles about being nice. Will you help me answer them?"

"Sure! We love riddles!" exclaimed Boots.

"All right, here's my first riddle," said the Troll.

"It was wrong to be grumpy to Mouse. I was very bad. What's the nice thing to say, so my friend won't be mad?"

"That's a great idea! I'll tell Mouse that I'm sorry!" cried the Grumpy Old Troll. "But I don't know where Mouse is," he continued sadly.

"We can check the Map," said Dora. "Say 'Map!'"

"I know how to find Mouse," said Map. "Mouse ran all the way back to his house. So you'll have to cross Sneezing Snake Lake, then go over Dragon Mountain, and that's how you'll get to Mouse's House."

Soon Dora, Boots, and the Troll arrived at the edge of Sneezing Snake Lake.

"How will we get across the lake?" wondered Boots.

Suddenly the Troll said,

"Look! It's Tico! And he's coming our way.
But how should I greet him? What's the nice thing to say?"

"Hello! *¡Hola,* Tico!" waved the Troll.
Tico offered to take Dora, Boots, and the
Troll across Sneezing Snake Lake in his boat.

They all put on life jackets and climbed aboard. Suddenly sneezing snakes started popping up!

"Achoo! Achoo!" sneezed the snakes.

"Oh, no!" said the Troll. "All this sneezing is making my nose tickle. I think I'm going to sneeze.

"I could sure use some more advice from you. When I have to sneeze, what should I do?"

Tico sailed the boat around all
the sneezing snakes.

Once they landed at the dock Dora, Boots, and the Troll jumped out of the boat.
The Troll said,

*"Tico got us across the lake lickety-split!
How do we let him know we appreciate it?"*

"¡*Gracias*, Tico!" called the Troll.
"¡*De nada!*" Tico replied as he sailed away.

"Where do we go next?" asked Boots.

"I know!" said the Troll. "We have to go over Dragon Mountain."

"Do you see anything that can take us over Dragon Mountain?" asked Boots.

The Troll saw an ice-cream truck driving up the road.

"Look! Our friend Val the octopus is driving that ice-cream truck. I bet she can take us over Dragon Mountain," Dora said.

"I remember what to do," said the Troll, and he called out, "*¡Hola!* Hello, Val!"

Val stopped the ice-cream truck, and they all climbed inside.

When they reached the top of Dragon Mountain, suddenly dragons jumped out and blocked the road.

"GO AWAY!" shouted the Troll.

But the dragons wouldn't budge.

"Hmm," said the Troll.

"Shouting won't scare these dragons away.
If I want them to move, what's the nice thing to say?"

"Please, dragons, will you move out of the way?" the Troll called.

"We're sorry!" the dragons replied. "We didn't mean to block the road. We just wanted some ice cream! Please? *¿Por favor?*"

"Sure!" said Val, and she handed everyone an ice-cream cone.

Soon Dora, Boots, and the Troll arrived at Mouse's House. The Troll knocked on the door.

"Mouse, please come out. I want to apologize," said the Troll.

Suddenly they heard a rustle coming from above.

"Look, it's Swiper! He's going to try and swipe our ice cream," said Boots.

"We have to stop Swiper," said Dora. "Say 'Swiper, no swiping!'"

"Oh Mannn!" said Swiper as he flew away.

"Hmmm," said the Troll, "I just learned something:

Swiping is not a nice thing to do.
If Swiper asked nicely, he could have ice cream too!"

Mouse opened the door and the Troll said, "I'm sorry I was grumpy. I was not a nice friend. Will you forgive me? Please? *¿Por favor?*"

Mouse was so happy to see the Troll that he said, "Yes! I forgive you!"

"Thank you! *¡Gracias!*" said the Troll.

"Hooray!" cheered Dora and Boots. "Mouse and the Troll are friends again! We did it!"

The Troll was so glad to play with his friends! He danced a happy dance as he said,

"*I learned many things on our trip.
You have to be nice if you want friendship.
Friends are helpful and caring and go out of their way.
So I'll be kind and polite—at least for today!*"